TALES FROM THE OTHER SIDE OF THE WORLD

stormgatepress.com
stormgatepress@gmail.com

Copyright © 2024 by Charles F. Millhouse
All rights reserved. This book or any portion thereof may not be reproduced or used in any manner whatsoever without the express written permission of the publisher except for the use of brief quotations in a book review or scholarly journal.
First Printing: 2024
ISBN: 9798304625043
Imprint: Independently published

Introducing the Stormgate Press Quick Read Books

Short Story Pulp Adventure Books
Reminiscent of the dime store novels of old.

BOOK 1: The Purple Mystique

BOOK 2: Night Vision

BOOK 3: A Zane Carrington Adventure

BOOK 4: The Purple Mystique: Purple Incognito

BOOK 5: Zane Carrington: The Contract

BOOK 6: Tales From the Other Side of the World: The Barbarian With No Name.

BOOK 7: Zane Carrington: Eternity's Time Clock

BOOK 8: Night Vision: Death Takes a Number (coming soon).

Watch for more books in the series coming soon...

Tales From the Other Side of the World
THE BARBARIAN WITH NO NAME

Charles F. Millhouse

The rider slowly steered his obsidian steed through the fire and ash of the burning village, the sign of hoof marks in the bloody soil made it clear that the slaughter was fresh and the men that did this were near.

As fate would have it, the fires pointed the way to the remains of the small settlement inside the Bragnor Forest. While the rider considered it luck, the people of this hamlet were anything but lucky. The empty eyes of decapitated heads stared blankly at him as he passed the victims. He had no remorse, no concern and in fact he had no feelings toward this mindless slaughter. For him it only meant he was one step closer to his destiny. If fate continued to be on his side, he would face the man responsible for this, the same man who robbed him of his most precious possession.

With his eyes shut, he sat tall in the saddle, allowing his senses to take control. His nostrils flared; his hearing acute. He left the confines of his mortal coil, focusing beyond his deerskin chinos, and chainmail chemise. The light wind on the air ruffled the bristles of his tightly trimmed beard and silvery hair. Though the smoke from the village, and the cracking of burning wood hampered his intuitive perception, his skills as a tracker prevailed. Call it foresight, or speculation, the rider sensed movement nearby.

The rider flung open his ashen eyes when he heard the pull of tightly strung leather. The bronze-skinned warrior shifted his weight in the saddle, and his well-trained mount understood his reaction and turned. A second later an arrow came out of the bellowing smolder and cut through the air – the ruffle from the feathers on the shaft, grazed the rider's right cheek. In the wake of the first arrow a second was released and snatched from the air into the man's oversized hand.

Breaking the arrow with little effort, he tossed it to the ground in a rage, as his hand went to the hilt of the broadsword at his back, he freed the instrument of war from its sheath and swung it freely at his side. "I don't know who you are," he called in haste. "But I'll have your blood on my blade before this day is done."

The ethereal form of a white skinned seraph came from the gray bristle, bow in hand and arrowed nocked. She wore the green skins of an animal – her downy hair woven at the back of her head. She moved forward with purpose. "You murdered them all," she exclaimed.

"Was not I who slaughtered this village," the rider claimed.

"Your army then," the warrior maiden asserted.

"Bold accusations, from someone so small." The rider retorted. "If it was an army at my command who did this, you would not be alive to sling arrows in my direction."

"You think me weak?"

"I think you dimwitted," the rider accused with a laugh in his words.

"So, you claim you're innocent?"

"I claim nothing, nor do I need to prove my innocence," the rider countered.

"Few enter the Bragnor Forest, and fewer still leave it unscathed," the woman said.

The rider's eyes thinned, he clenched his jaw and reared back on the reins as he kicked the side of his horse with resolve. He had no more time for banter, a far greater deed was upon him. As he rode past the warrior fair, glancing down on her, their eyes locked onto one another, as she whispered, "Do your past transgressions outweigh that which is noble in your soul, Barbarian?"

Before the rider knew what was happening, he was whisked from the battle-torn village, his body jerked backward, back to many months hence. To another time, another place. When he was no barbarian at all, but a husband, a statesmen and a general.

His mind clouded to a life destroyed. Caught in the moment of ceremony, when he rode through the streets of Shimma, the capital of the Dorvainian Empire. The crowds cheered for him, rose petals rained down on him, and the people of the city worshiped him. They would call his name, General Sandar... General Sandar ... General Sandar... they would applaud his triumphs, and they would honor him to the point that even some would say he was more popular than good King Xon.

Onward through the capital he rode – the banners of the empire accompanied him, the sound of trumpets heralded his arrival, and as his horse trotted through the main gates of the castle, the General waved toward the masses, regaling them with one final wave as the ramparts closed behind him.

One of the King's guards called, "All hail, General…"

"Enough," the General called with a raised hand. "Enough. I have to endure the admiration from the populace, must I suffer it within the walls of the castle as well?" he asked.

Dismounting his steed, the General was met by his squire, who began to release the armor around his midsection. "The people of the empire have placed me on a pedestal," the General mumbled. He looked at his frail squire and said, "I am just a man who has fought some wars and defended the people as best I could. I don't desire their praise, nor do I deserve it."

"Yes, my General," the timid squire replied in a subservient tone.

"Have my horse tended to and see there is a barrel of wine waiting for me within the hour," the General ordered as he crossed the quad, only to be stopped by a tall lanky man in long purple and yellow silk robes. "Uh, Keffa, you slimy toad. I only see you when your master is indisposed. So, tell me, what does that irrepressible charlatan, want you to tell me?"

TALES FROM THE OTHER SIDE OF THE WORLD

"Master Grenvere did not send me my General. I am here at bequest of King Xon. He expects you in the throne room at once."

The General thought of his wife. His desires for a warm bath, her warm soul and a tankard of warm mead superseded his loyalty for his king, but it didn't overshadow his honor. Even though he found the allegiance of the people annoying, he understood his part to play. To ignore his king was to ignore the people.

"Should I tell King Xon you will be coming?" Keffa asked.

"I do not need you to lead the way, toad," the General said. "I will see the king *now*."

The throne room of King Xon's fortress was a testimony of brutal power and raw strength. Hewn from dark stone, the walls were adorned with the hides of fierce beasts and the banners of conquered tribes. Flickering torches cast eerie shadows across the room, highlighting the rough-hewn pillars that supported the ceiling. At the far end, on a raised dais, sat King Xon on a massive throne carved from the bones of ancient leviathans. The throne was draped with the pelts of dire wolves, and the king himself, a towering figure of muscle and scarred flesh. Gripping the armrests with hands that have seen countless battles he leaned forward when the General entered the massive chamber.

"Tell me General of your battle," Xon said. "Tell me of the blood, smoke and fires you waged against our enemy, for I long to be among the fight."

Beside the king, lurking in the shadows, was Grenvere, the King's sorcerer. Grenvere was a gaunt figure, draped in tattered robes that seem to writhe with a life of their own, the air around him crackled with dark magic and his cold, calculating stare never left the General.

"My king," the General said with a bow at the foot of the throne. "The battle at the Black Gorge was hard-fought. We crushed the enemy's vanguard, but their reinforcements took us by surprise. We held the line, but at great cost."

Leaning forward, Xon said with pride in his tone, "Your warriors are the finest in the realm. I trust your judgment and understand lives must be lost to secure the empire. Tell me, what of our triumphs? Tell me of our gained territories. They are plentiful?"

"Aye, my lord. We have taken the western plateau and secured the river crossings. The lands there are fertile and will provide for our armies. However, the losses were heavy, and we need time to regroup."

Nodding, Xon leaned back and steepled his fingers. "Good. Good," he said in a pleasing tone. "The western plateau will strengthen our hold on the region. And the defeats?"

The General grimaced, and with heavy words said, "The ambush at Blood Pass was a bitter blow. We underestimated their numbers and their resolve. Many of our warriors fell, but we managed to retreat and save the rest."

Grenvere stepped from the shadows, sneering, and said, "Perhaps if our esteemed general had heeded my warnings, the outcome might have been different."

Glaring at Grenvere, the General grumbled, "Your warnings were nothing but vague mutterings, sorcerer. My warriors fight with steel and blood, not with shadows and whispers."

King Xon held up a hand to silence them, and said, "Enough, General. I understand your hatred for Grenvere, but his counsel has its uses. We must combine our strengths if we are to conquer our enemies."

The General eyed Grenvere. The sorcerer had become weak as of late. His skin had paled, his hair had thinned, and his eyes weren't as sharp as before. With someone wielding as much power as Grenvere, perhaps even he could not defeat death. "What do you hope to achieve Sorcerer? Adulation from the people? You rarely show your face outside the castle. Wealth? You conjure up everything that you need. Power, *yes* power. All men desire it and I dare say *you* even more so. But what kind of power Grenvere? Absolute power, or the kind that is built in the shadows?"

The sorcerer stepped back into the dim light behind the throne offering a wily grin.

"Yes, of course, I might have known," the General said reaching for the broadsword strapped to his back. "Perhaps I should put an end to any scheme you might be concocting."

"Enough!" King Xon protested. "You dare unsheathe your weapon in my presence. I could have your head for such an act alone."

The General eyed Grenvere, and for an instant, the idea that the sorcerer had vexed the king weighed heavy on him.

"I beg your forgiveness, Sire. I have no excuse for my actions."

"I daresay," Xon spat out. "But I will overlook this transgression because of your loyalty to the empire and to me. But let it be known General that while I consider you a trustworthy ally, I feel the same about Grenvere. You will respect him, as *I* respect him, and as I respect you."

"As you command, my king," the General said. "But know this sorcerer: I trust my sword and my men more than your sorceries of this..."

"And I trust that your sword will find its mark, General. If it does not, we all face ruin," Xon said. "Prepare your men for the next campaign."

"If I may be so bold, Sire. What campaign will that be?" the General asked. "I know of nothing else threating the empire at this time."

"I shall keep those plans close to my heart, General... for now." Xon said with a reluctance in his tone. "Grenvere and I are still devising the war, and we'll share it in good time."

It was the only time during the conversation that the General felt that the King's words were forced and not his own. He eyed the sorcerer and replaced the sword into its sheath, saying, "As you wish, my King. We will not fail."

Grenvere whispered, "For your sake, General, I hope you speak the truth. The King desires loyalty above all."

For an instant the General thought about unleashing his sword for a second time, *Death's Edge,* would drink the sorcerer's blood a plenty. As he left the throne room, the tension between him and the sorcerer were undeniable. The flickering torches cast long shadows, hinting at the struggles and battles yet to come. Though he didn't know what kind of battle it would be, he was sure there was something amiss inside the castle and before long, he would uncover it, and blood would flow.

***

The bathwater was a soothing cocoon, warm and inviting, but the presence of Lasha made it intoxicating. She lay draped against Sandar, her bare skin smooth and supple, her body pressed tightly against his. Her firm breasts pressed against his chest, igniting his senses. He let his fingers trail through her thick, raven hair, feeling the silky strands slip between his fingers as he traced his way down to her cheek. His hand lingered there, caressing her delicate features, absorbing the heat radiating from her skin.

Their lips met, the kiss slow at first but quickly deepening as passion took hold. Lasha's soft moans spilled into his ear, each one a tantalizing whisper that stirred something primal within him. Her breath mingled with his, warm and rapid, as they moved in unison, enveloped in the warmth of the water and the undeniable heat of each other's embrace. The world outside faded away, leaving only the two of them in a haven of intimacy and desire.

The water crashed the side of the tub in waves of ecstasy, their thrusts of pleasure built to an uncontrollable climax, as they spilled upon one another, their breathing labored but controlled as they enjoyed the moment as if it would never come again.

Despite their intense lovemaking, Lasha's expression was one of concern. She silently regarded her husband – their eyes locked in quiet conversation. "You are concerned, Drapa," she said. "I do not have to hear you say it, to understand something is wrong."

Sandar sat up in the bath, and he spoke with honesty, "The King is seeking another war."

"With whom?" Lasha asked.

"I cannot say, because I do not know," Sandar said. "I fear he is vexed by Grenvere, and the sorcerer is convincing him to spread to the east."

"There is no threat from there," Lasha said with certainty. "Only farmers and a splattering of villages in and around the Bragnor Forest. Beyond that, no one knows for sure."

Sandar thought for a time and said, "It is said that Grenvere is from beyond the Bragnor Forest. That his people are there."

"What are you saying?" Lasha asked and she moved to the other side of the tub.

Sandar stepped out of the water, grabbing a towel. Their bath chamber sat atop their Chateau along the mountainside overlooking the city. "The people cheer to me. Call me a hero," he said. "I think that snake Grenvere is jealous."

"What do you mean, jealous," Lasha said as she too climbed out of the cooling water, wrapping herself in an oversized towel. "He is nowhere the man you are... few men are, my husband."

"That's what I'm talking about. If Grenvere was a normal man, I would not give it a second thought. But he's not a normal man. He has power and influence and it's difficult to discern what he could do with it."

"I fear you worry for no reason," Lasha said as she took her towel and began to dry Sandar. She moved down, dabbing his legs.

Taking Lasha by the wrists, and pulling her up to look in her eyes, he said, "If a man could love a woman as much as I, there would be no wars in this world."

"There is no man, who loves a woman more than you," Lasha replied. "All things will come to pass, my husband."

"I hope you are correct," Sandar said. "But for a long while now, I've sensed a darkness covering the land, and I can't fight the feeling that it's Grenvere at the center of it."

Lasha wrapped her arms around Sandar's strong body and said, "For tonight put it out of your mind, my husband. Come, take me to bed. I will keep your mind occupied for the night. Tomorrow you can worry about the king, about Grenvere and about the people of the empire. But for now, for me, I seek strength of your arms, the tenderness of your hands and the feel of your manhood inside me."

Sandar scooped Lasha up into his arms, they shared a quiet look as he carried her into the adjoining room, and onto their downy bed.

***

The next day, as the sun hung low in the sky, casting long shadows across the training field, Sandar stood with his arms crossed, watching his men spar. The clashing of steel and the grunts of exertion filled the air, but despite the noise and the heat of the day, a cold unease crawled along his spine. He couldn't shake the feeling that someone, or something, was watching him.

His eyes scanned the perimeter of the field, over the weathered wooden barriers, and toward the dense trees lining the edge of the camp. The birds, usually loud and chirping, were eerily silent. A faint rustle in the underbrush caught his attention, but when he turned toward it, all he saw was the waving grass, empty and still.

Sandar's grip tightened on the hilt of his sword, though he made no motion to draw it. The men around him were oblivious to the mounting tension, too focused on their training to notice. A warrior was taught to be alert, to sense the unseen, and his instincts screamed that something was wrong. He looked to his right, where Sigrin, his second-in-command, was standing tall with his hands resting on the pommel of his axe. Sandar's eyes locked with Sigrin's, and for a brief moment, the unspoken understanding passed between them: something wasn't right.

The feeling intensified as the minutes stretched on, a gnawing presence that seemed to follow his every move. He resisted the urge to look over his shoulder, knowing it would reveal nothing but the same empty stretch of the training ground. Still, the sensation grew stronger. His heart picked up its rhythm, steady yet anticipating. The air was heavy, thick with the promise of something that might break at any moment.

Then, as if to challenge his instincts, a faint whisper seemed to brush against his ear, so soft he might have imagined it. But Sandar wasn't a man given to superstition, but he was a man well aware of sorcery. His mind was sharp, his senses honed. There was no denying it now: they were not alone.

His hand tightened his sword, steeping forward, into the center of the field, raising his voice for the first time that day. "Form up!" His men immediately snapped to attention, their eyes darting toward him, confused by the sudden change in his demeanor.

"That's all for today," he said receiving odd looks from his men. "I know it isn't our normal training session, but warriors must be as sharp as their steel. Take the day off, find a tankard of ale, the body of a woman and pass the day in their embrace."

The men agreed with laughter and roaring applause. "Now, go," Sandar insisted. "Tomorrow we will return to training, but be prepared to be sharpened, battle ready and tested to your fullest."

As the men broke ranks, Sandar was approached by Sigrin. "You're on edge, General," he said with worry in his tone.

"I am concerned for the King," Sandar said, his voice low and guarded.

"In what way?" Sigrin asked.

Sandar didn't have an answer. All he had was speculation. He forced a smile on his lips, and said, "Do not allow my misgivings to concern you, old friend. It simply might be the musings of an old man. Nothing more. Now go, eat, drink, for tomorrow we live another day."

Sigrin clapped his chest with his fist and with hand on the hilt of his weapon, he turned and left the training field.

Sandar eyed the blue sky above. He longed for the days of peace, and when he understood what the world meant to him. His king was bewitched, his army depleted, and his own mortality stared him square in the eye. *What will become of this land when I am no more?"* he asked himself.

"General," a voice called from across the training field, and Sandar turned to find two of the palace guards in their silver and gold fineries approach him. Their strides with purpose, and their eyes sharp with intent.

"The King summons you, Sandar."

"That's General Sandar," he replied, even though the palace guard did not fall under his command, he sought respect from anyone in the King's employ.

The guards' expressions didn't alter, and they waited for him to accompany them. *Were these the ones watching me?* Sandar wondered but dismissed that idea quickly. He eyed the two men, their resolves focused, their orders engrained.

"I do not require guards to escort me. I know my way," Sandar said as he turned. The idea that the General of the King's army should be treated in such a manner infuriated him. He wondered what the palace guards would have done if he refused to go with them. There would be no challenge. They posed no threat, and Sandar did not care to put his theory to a test. Instead, he led the way with the guards one step behind.

The King sat on his throne much as he did the day before when Sandar entered the throne room. In fact, the King's attire was the same as he wore the day before – he never knew the King to be so disheveled. The chamber was empty except for a handful of guards, and some ladies in waiting. The General never knew the great hall so devoid of people when the King was in attendance.

"Ah, General," Xon said in a pleasant recognition as Sandar approached.

Sandar bent to a knee when he stopped at the foot of his king. "I live to serve," he said. As he raised his gaze, he saw Grenvere lurking behind the great chair. A bitter taste came to his mouth, and he stood on the King's bidding.

"This is an auspicious occasion, General," Xon said leaning forward in his chair slightly.

"Is that so, Sire?" Sandar asked.

"Prepare your army to march within seven days hence," Xon said with a sense of delight in his voice.

"March, march where, Sire?" Sandar asked.

"You will secure our borders to the east," the King said with satisfaction. "You will secure the lands, the villages, the people and recruiting new citizens into your army as you go."

To say Sandar was surprised by the King's words would have been misleading. He knew the time was coming, only, he hoped he was wrong. "We have no quarrel with the people in the lands of the east, my King," he said trying to understand the command. "Why would we do such a thing?"

"My empire cannot truly be an empire without every soul under my rule," Xon declared, his voice resonating with an almost unearthly authority that gave the throne room a wintery chill. His eyes, however, told a different story. They were hollow, lifeless... two empty wells that gave no hint of humanity, as if whatever spirit once fueled him had been siphoned away, leaving only a shell that moved and spoke but did not feel.

Sandar, standing before the king, forced himself to meet that void, feeling a chill run through him. He understood what Xon was asking, and what it would mean. His whole life had been devoted to the king, his purpose carved into his soul like stone: to serve, to execute his will, no matter the cost. But this order, this vision of a relentless, consuming empire, stirred a shadow of doubt he dared not voice.

Xon studied him, his gaze a heavy weight. "You will see that the peoples of the east understand their place, as you march, General," Xon continued, a cruel smile tugging at his lips. His words were a command, but Sandar heard the deeper threat beneath them, a warning to any who faltered.

Sandar drew in a breath, half-prepared to respond but finding his voice caught in his throat. The loss of so many lives, entire lands swallowed in blood and fire for the sake of the empire. He could feel it tearing at him, loosening the very foundation of his loyalty. And yet, how could he question the man who had united the Western lands, brought peace to warring tribes, and lifted his name to greatness? Xon did not wage war for greed or vanity, but to secure his realm, to crush any who would stand against his unyielding rule.

"My Lord, wouldn't it be wiser to send an emissary to speak for you, rather than my blade?" Sandar asked. "Their people mean us no ill-will."

"Why do you hesitate, General?" Xon asked, his voice softening, almost taunting, as a glint of something dark and knowing crossed his hollow gaze.

"I merely wish to spare any unneeded bloodshed," Sandar said.

"You are a warrior!" Xon exclaimed. "You kill when I order it, that is your purpose."

"I mean no disrespect, Sire," Sandar said. "But we are a nation of strength, not of gratuitous violence. It has never been your way."

"Ways change, General. Men change. I have changed," Xon said.

"Or you have been forced to change," Sandar muttered in a whisper.

"What did you say?" Xon demanded.

Sandar shifted his gaze, and saw the snake, Grenvere lurking nearby. That's when he realized, the King was truly bewitched. The sorcerer not only had his ear, but by some unnatural power, the King fell to Grenvere's magic.

Sandar stormed forward, his hands clenched into fists. "What have you done to him *snake?*" he demanded. "Whatever it was, you will release him, or I will carve you open like a stuck pig."

Suddenly, shadows engulfed the throne room as the great, towering windows were slowly obscured, inch by inch, by massive iron bands that creaked and groaned into place, sealing out the last glimmers of daylight. A hollow boom echoed through the chamber as the heavy main door slammed shut, sending a shudder through the floor. The sound resonated ominously, final and unyielding, as if sealing a tomb. Within moments, a second barrier descended over the door, thick, impenetrable, and lined with glistening steel rivets that glinted in the fading light, forming a wall as solid as a fortress.

The room plunged into near darkness, save for the faint, flickering glow of torches that lined the walls. Shadows stretched and twisted, wrapping around the columns and creeping along the floor like specters, casting the chamber in an eerie half-light that seemed to press in on all sides. The air grew thick, almost suffocating, as if the very walls were closing in, and a cold silence settled over the room. A silence that felt unnatural, deliberate, cast into place by Grenvere's dark magic.

In the stifling gloom, Sandar turned slowly toward the throne, every instinct within him screaming to flee. But the King's voice shattered the silence – a menacing laughter that began as a low, ominous rumble, growing louder and more twisted with every passing second. The sound filled the chamber like a storm, dark and all-consuming. From the shadows beside the throne, Grenvere stepped forward, his face split into a mocking grin as he echoed the King's laughter, a hollow mimicry that sent a shiver down Sandar's spine.

But then Xon's laughter took on a savage edge, escalating in pitch until it felt as though it might shake the very walls. At that moment, Grenvere raised his hands and began to chant in a language dark and ancient, his words dripping with a sinister energy. His voice echoed off the stone walls, filled with a weight and purpose that was almost palpable. "Novac, notoria, ifrom, doniel," he intoned, each syllable resonating with a power that seemed to thicken the air, pulling shadows tighter around the room.

Suddenly, Grenvere's gaze locked onto Sandar, and with a cruel smile, he thrust a long, bony finger in his direction. "Sanctum – moretallus!" he roared, each word laden with dark intent, his voice cracking like thunder as he unleashed the final syllable.

An invisible force exploded outward from Grenvere's hand, striking Sandar with the power of a tidal wave. The sheer impact drove him backward, his heels skidding across the stone floor as he fought to steady himself. His body shuddered under the force, a wave of searing energy pulsing through him as though it might tear him apart from within. The room swam before his eyes, and for a heartbeat, he felt his very essence being tugged, as though some dark power sought to claim him.

Sandar righted himself, his head dizzy and his vision hazy. Through clouded vision, he saw the transformation happen. The weak timid sorcerer stood erect, his shape augmenting, his figure towering and changing, his muscles growing and taking shape, his hair growing, and a newly form beard shading his face. "This isn't possible..." Sandar said as he stared at the new regenerated Grenvere, as he stared at himself.

Another force of power came from Grenvere, and before Sandar could react it slammed into him, sending him for a spiral until he slammed to the floor – the force of the power knocked him out.

***

Sandar woke in the dungeon, stripped of his clothes, he dangled by his wrists naked. There was very little light, and he heard voices nearby. "Who's there," he demanded. His voice was hoarse, and throat sore. "This is General Sandar, I swear I'll have your heads on pikes for treating me such."

"They don't care who you are," a voice came from the dark.

"Who's there?" Sandar asked.

"I am me," the voice said. "And you are you."

"I am General Drapa Sandar," he said.

"Is, is that supposed to be someone important?" the bodyless voice asked. A faint laugh lingered in his words. "No one cares who you are." The form of a skeletal looking man came from the shadows. He too was naked, but he managed to find a piece of filthy deerskin to cover himself. "When you come down here, no one cares who you are. You are forgotten about. You'll be lucky if you eat more than two times in a week. And you'll never, never see sunlight again."

Sandar struggled with his bindings; the strength left his arms, and he lost all feeling in them. "How long have you been down here old man?" he asked.

The gaunt man thought for a moment. His eyes were inset in his head, and what hair that remained atop his head strung in his eyes. "All my life," he finally answered.

Sandar considered the man was speaking nonsense. It seemed as if his mind faded long before his body. "What did you do, to be sentenced to an existence down in this shithole?"

"When you speak out against the royal family, this is where they send you," the old skinny man replied. "I pray to Dorma, asking the goddess to free me from this worldly life, but she does not answer. She has forsaken me."

Sandar considered that Dorma did not answer, because she is not real. If the gods ever did exist, they have forsaken this world long ago. "When do they bring the food down here?" he asked. Even now the General was devising a way to escape.

Testing his bravery, the thin man moved nearer toward Sandar, and with a sinewy finger he pointed at the general and said, "It's hard to tell. Like I said food is few and far between down here, and then you have to fight for it, and as you see, I am but a shadow of what I used to be."

Sandar didn't have time to hang here. Soon Sigrin would come concerned over his disappearance, *but would he know to look down here?*" he asked himself. "Guard," he bellowed. "Guard, I demand you come here at once!"

The old man cackled. "It won't help. The guards never come; they don't care. They don't intervene when the men fight, and they care even less when the women down here are raped."

"Women? There are women down here?" Sandar hissed.

"Anyone who opposes the King or speaks out against Grenvere is cast down here."

"*Grenvere*," Sandar snarled. "When I get my hands on him, I'll snap his neck and feed him to the pigs."

"Many men have said the same thing," the old man said. "But none ever get the chance. Just the utterance of his name sends the guards into a frenzy."

"Why?" Sandar inquired.

The old man just stared at Sandar as if he too were afraid to bring the wrath of the guards down on him.

"It's alright, old man. I won't let anyone harm you."

The frail man regarded Sandar and offered a painful smile. His rotten teeth filled his mouth. "Brave words for a man who is hung up like the morning catch."

Sandar's gaze shot aloft studying his binds. The ropes that held him were tight, and even though it was dark in the cavern, he could tell that there was no blood in his hands. His strength was spent, and if he didn't act soon, he would have none to fight his way out. Perhaps that was how they beat their prisoners into submission, but allowing time to whittle away their fortitude. He could not allow that to happen, and he had to get out, *now*.

"Guards...! You belly filled sons of whores, Guards...!"

The old man waved his gaunt hands in front of him, and offered a warning, "You bring down the wrath of the entire dungeon on all of us, if you keep this up."

"Oh, I'm just getting started," Sandar admitted. Raising his voice even louder, he shouted, "Any son of a dog that takes orders from that charlatan, Grenvere is either a coward, or too stupid to think for themselves...!"

A moment later footfalls could be heard clomping toward the cell door. "See, see, you've done it, you'll be beat for such insolence."

Sandar didn't offer a reply. Instead, he started to build up strength in his arm and legs. He would only get one chance at this – but one chance would be all he needed.

"What piece of filth can't keep their mouth shut," an earless man with an oversized flat nose, and small beady eyes asked as he unlocked the cell door.

"Was not I, was not I," the old man pleaded when the cell door squealed open.

"I know it's not you Grendo," the guard said in a nasally tone. "We broke you a long time ago. No, no it's our new guest, who needs to be shown the proper respect."

"I am General Drapa Sandar, I demand you release me, now."

The guard grunted a laugh. "A general says you, a barbarian says I. Otherwise why would you be down here with me, and the likes of him?" he said pointing at Grendo.

Sandar didn't wait another second. With lightning speed, he lifted himself up, wrapping his bare legs around the guard's neck. The guard struggle, but Sandar's strength was too much for him as the general pulled the guard tight against his manhood, and using the man's body as leverage, he lifted himself up and off the hook that imprisoned him.

Blood coursed through his arms once again and stung his appendages with little sharp needles. Kicking the guard away with the heel of his foot, Sandar pulled the man's scabbard from his belt and drove it into the guard's neck. Covering the dying man's mouth, he held on until the body stopped writhing.

"Look what you did," Grendo said in surprised adulation.

Sandar withdrew, looking for his clothes, but the old man told him, "You were brought in this way."

Eyeing the dead guard, he studied the man's chain mailed tunic and pulled it off his body. Dressing himself in the rest of the guard's clothes, he armed himself with only the scabbard and headed out of the cage, but he stopped and turned towards the old man and said, "You're free, you can go."

"Been here a long time," Grendo said. "I resigned that I would die in this place, and I tend too. There is nothing outside for me anymore, *nothing.* Go barbarian, you haven't much time."

Sandar didn't hesitate and bolted out of the cell. His thoughts were of killing the sorcerer, watching him die the most horrible of deaths pleased him, but that would have to wait. If he was imprisoned, then where was Lasha, his wife? What did Grenvere do to her? His heart raced with fear as he ran into the night air.

Fires had been set throughout the city as night fell on the capital. Guardsmen patrolled the streets, and as of yet, no alarms rung warning of his escape. Finding his way into the residential district he stalked stealthily keeping to the shadows and not drawing attention to himself. Soon the streets would be crawling with soldiers seeking him out. The idea that his name did not carry weight within the prison did not concern him, not yet. All he worried about was Lasha and was she safe.

If any woman in the city could protect herself, it would be her. Sandar taught her how to handle a sword, how to protect herself even against the strongest man. Even though his wife was formidable it was unlikely she could defend herself against a horde of attackers. Sandar's heart palpitated uncontrollably.

His home rested halfway up a mountainside, overlooking the city. There were no other homes near it, and as he approached, he didn't worry about being seen. Torches burned along the perimeter, and there were a few servants throughout the dwelling, but he chose to not make his presence known as he entered the chalet.

The odor of sweet wine and cooking antelope filled the home, and the beast inside Sandar's stomach growled to be fed. The meal was his favorite, and Lasha always had it fixed the night before he prepared to ride on a new campaign. This didn't settle well with him, but he put that thought out of his mind for now. He wouldn't rest until he saw his wife, held her in his arms.

Ascending the stairwell up to their private quarters, Sandar entered the well-lit chamber, the smell of her perfume mixing with that of the meal downstairs. He moved quietly, his senses urging him toward the bathhouse where he found the oversized tub filled with water, and lavender aromatics. He tested the water with his hand. *Cold,* and he turned quickly when he heard the unmistakable sound of a sword being released from its sheath.

He stood facing his wife, all she wore was her silk robe barely hiding her slender form; the nipples of her ample breasts showing through the material. Rage gripped her features, and she demanded, "Who are you, why are you here?"

Taken aback, Sandar was at a loss for words. "Lasha...?"

"How dare you use my name as though we are familiar," she hissed. She charged ahead with the very sword he gave her. Forged and balanced to match her form. She used the attack he taught her and handled the blade with precision. If he didn't know the move himself, it would have been deadly.

Tossing the scabbard to the floor he chose to defend himself weaponless, shifting his body at the last second allowing the blade to pass by him – he snagged her sword arm using his body as leverage, he offered enough pressure causing her to drop the weapon to the wooden floor below.

Using her sharp fingernails as a weapon, Lasha tore into Sandar's arm, hissing like a cat. With a delicate push, he knocked her back, and he turned to face her. "Lasha, it's me, it's Drapa."

Lasha paused and took a step back. "You lie," she shouted. "My husband left an hour ago, to return to the King, and prepare for the march tomorrow."

"March... the march east," Sandar said.

Lasha didn't offer a reply.

"Lasha, I don't know what has happened, but I swear to you, I am your husband, I am Drapa Sandar, general of the King's army, protector of the Empire, first soldier of the army of Dorvainia."

Stupefied, Lasha stood speechless, studying him. Sandar took a step toward her, and she backed away.

Not breaking eye contact with Lasha, Sandar kept his tone level, and said, "If a man could love a woman as much as I, there would be no wars in this world."

Lasha gasped and with destress in her tone, she replied, "There is no man, who loves a woman more than you."

"If only they could try," Sandar said.

"It is you, my husband," Lasha said. "Though I do not know how. You look... look not as yourself."

Sandar saw his image in a mirror on the wall. To him, he looked like himself – the same gray beard, the same flowing hair. "That rat, Grenvere," he said enraged. "His dark magic has cursed me and changed my appearance so I appear different to others. He has stolen my life, my name."

Lasha took a step back, a look of horror etched on her features. "I took him to our bed, my husband," she said.

Sandar wasn't surprised. The smell of the dinner when he entered the home, the water in the tub, and the wet footprints leading into their bedroom. He eyed her and said, "You were deceived, there is nothing to be ashamed of."

"If he has taken your identity, your face that means..."

"He controls my army, and he tends to wage war on the unsuspecting lands of the east," Sandar said. He turned toward the balcony and gazed upon the city. When he turned back toward Lasha, he said, "I'll have that swine on the end of a sword before this night is out."

The city felt different, Sandar didn't know how to explain it, only that the life had gone out of the world, and the people of Shimma felt it too. Besides some vagrants on the street, the General was alone as he made his way toward the castle. Despite there not being any sentries about, the closer he went toward the King's Keep the more opposition he would encounter. Still, he didn't fret. He trained most of the men guarding the castle, even though they didn't fall under his authority, there might be a few loyal to him. If the dark sorcerer had taken his appearance, it might be more of a challenge to convince them who was who. The soonER he could put his blade in Grenvere the better.

27

When footfalls clamored through the cobblestone streets, Sandar got a suspicious feeling he was wrong. Screams echoed as the march came closer toward him and soon, he was met with fleeing citizens their horror-stricken faces told him all he needed to know.

Grabbing the arm of a woman, Sandar pulled into the shadows of a building, and said, "What it is woman, what frightens you?"

The woman's eyes scanned Sandar's face, but she didn't recognize him. like his wife, the woman was seeing General Drapa Sandar, the most famous man in all of the Dorvainian Empire, as a stranger. He increased his grip, and throwing anger into his tone, he said, "Tell me woman."

"The city guards have been ordered by the King himself to search every home, every inn and to imprison every man over thirty," she said, horror lacing her tone.

"Devil dogs," Sandar hissed as he released the woman to continue on her way. Grenvere couldn't issue an order to kill General Sandar, considering the sorcerer was using his features and the guards didn't know who they were looking for.

More screams came from up the street, and Sandar had little choice. He could stop and fight the guards, but there would be a chance one of the men he trained would get lucky and deliver a devastating blow.

As much as he hated turning his back on the citizens of Shimma, he had to get to the castle, had to take Grenvere's head and finish this, *now... this moment.*

The entryway to the castle was well guarded, and by Sandar's surprise, it was his own men – Soldiers of the

King's Army. They never stood guard. *Never.* They were always training, always preparing to protect the empire, never reduced to something as trivial as standing guard.

Grenvere was afraid, afraid he would fail before he could march the army on a campaign of death and destruction, and... Sandar stumbled in his thoughts and hid in the shadows watching the men at the gate. Something was not right. Their movements were as if they were made of wood, like puppets on hidden strings. Then he saw it, they were repeating every movement precisely as they did before. His men were well trained, but not to the point every facial expression, every movement of a hand, every blink of an eye happened in order every ninety seconds. *It's an illusion,* Sandar told himself. *They're not real.*

With the King's guard rampaging through the city looking for him, the castle was left unguarded. But if these men were not his, then where was his army. His stomach hit rock bottom. They were marching east, just as Grenvere intended.

Breaking his cover, Sandar pulled his sword and headed toward the front gate of the castle. If these were his men, if they indeed were real, they would overwhelm him, and it was certain he would die.

Approaching the guards, they didn't flinch, nor did they look in his direction. Their movements continued just as they had when Sandar approached. Over and over again. When Sandar walked right through them, the illusions faded, flickering like candles in the wind. Entering the castle's keep, echoes haunted the citadel. The hollow sound of emptiness filled every corner of the quadrangle and all he heard were ghosts of the past.

If his army was gone, and the King's Guard hellbent throughout the city, then the castle, in fact the very empire was unprotected. Sprinting up the long stone stairs toward the inter sanctum, Sandar's horrors were realized when he entered the throne room, to find the once strong image of King Xon, now reduced to a vestige of decay and despair. His haggard form slumped on his throne, his once dark beard, turned gray and wiry.

"Milord," Sandar said on approach. "What vexes you?"

"You look like you've seen a ghost, General," Xon said, but his tone seemed different, as if it were not his own.

"Milord?"

Xon broke out in rancid laughter, his bloodshot eyes glistened with tears as if he was trying not to weep.

"Sire?" Sandar bent down close to the King; he placed a hand atop of Xon's only to feel the touch of death. Jerking his hand away, he exclaimed, "What madness is this...?"

"You're a fool, General," Xon said, but his voice was not his, but Grenvere's.

Sandar stumbled back, his sword pulled up preparing to strike. "You truly are the devil," he hissed.

"The devil has nothing on me, General," Grenvere said with a slippery smile. "I control the King, your army and I even took your wife in your very bed. There is nothing you can do to stop me now."

For a split second, Sandar thought about running his blade into Xon's chest. If only to free him from the torment, but he stilled his hand. "If you can hear me, Milord, I swear to you I will not rest until you, and all of Dorvainia is free." He leaned in close to the chair, his eyes looking into the King's but all he saw was the insidious gaze of Grenvere. "Know this sorcerer, I am coming for you, and when we meet next, I will take your head."

Sandar marched from the throne room determined. His sole purpose in life was to find and kill the man who stole his life, his wife, and his king. He would do whatever he needed to do, to bring an end to Grenvere's tyranny, if it took him the rest of his life, he would see it done.

Images faded around him, the tic of the clock spring forward, and his life spun out of control, the voice of the warrior maiden filled his mind, and drew him back to the instant she entered his mine... "Do your past transgressions outweigh that which is noble in your soul, Barbarian?"

He jerked back, the force of some powerful mind attack reeled, and he lost his balance, falling from his horse and striking the ground with a tremendous thud. He was back in the Bragnor Forest, he tried to comprehend the time since he rode away from Shimma, to when he entered the forest. A fortnight, if not more – time was meaningless to him now. Only the death of Grenvere was all that mattered.

"You speak the truth," the warrior woman said as she bent over Sandar. "You did not attack us."

"It took you splitting open my mind like a cantaloupe to realize this?" Sandar asked. "How did you... you're a sorceress...!"

"Nothing so inspiring," the young woman said with certainty. "I am a Sprite, my skills are more of the bow and axe." She patted the petite axe strapped to her waist. "But like all of my kind, I have a limited practitioner's aptitude."

"What the hell does that mean?"

"I..." the Sprite hesitated and withdrew. She stood erect, tilting her head to one side like a mischievous puppy. "We are not alone," she said.

Soldiers appeared from the thick foliage around the destroyed village. Weapons in hand, they stood ready, their gazes focused on Sandar and his companion. He knew them in an instant. These were his men, handpicked by him to fight for the honor of the Dorvainian Empire.

When Sigrin stepped forward, Sandar turned to face him. "You are under arrest, by orders of General Drapa Sandar," he said.

Sandar tried to think of something to say, something that his second in command would hear and recognize him even though he no longer looked like the man he knew. "You don't have to do this," he said.

"Barbarians are outlaws in the Dorvainian Empire," Sigrin said.

"But we are not in the empire," Sandar said.

"The empire is wherever the King's flags fly," Sigrin said.

Sandar had said that many times in the past to bestow a since of pride in his men. he never thought it would come back against him. "I refuse your authority," he said eyeing the men surrounding him. He would not be able to fight them all and he really didn't stomach the idea of killing his own men.

"My general thought you would say that," Sigrin replied. "You leave me no choice."

"We all have a choice, Commander, if we take time to use our minds more than our weapons."

Sigrin hesitated. He regarded Sandar with a curious eye. "Have we met before?" he asked.

"No matter what I told you, you wouldn't believe it," Sandar said. "But I am still not going with you."

"Then I have to do my duty," Sigrin said. "Take the barbarian, I don't care what you do with the girl."

At that instant, the Sprite shifted her feet, taking a battle stance, her small axe in hand. Sandar glanced at her, and then at his men. "Is that the honor of a warrior of Dorvainia? He asked.

"We are on a conquest, ordained by our King, and our General has given us carte blanche to do with prisoners as we will, and *she* is the prettiest prisoner we've seen in a long time."

At that moment, Sandar knew these were no longer his men. He trained them to follow orders, and even though he hoped their reckless attitude was a part of one of Grenvere's wicked spells, he couldn't allow them to take him or hurt the Sprite. "Come at us then," Sandar said. "The day is short, and so are your lives."

The soldiers charged and Sandar pushed the Sprite back out of the way, to her verbal protest. He drew back his broadsword, and although it was not his, he would wield the weapon as he would any other. To meet his enemy in mortal combat. He put the idea out of his mind that these were his men as he prepared to bloody his blade with their blood.

Steel clashed against steel. The strikes were precise, and Sandar's targets were taken apprehensively. He did not revel in the deaths of his men, and when he faced his second in command, he and Sigrin were evenly matched. They countered one another's attacks with ease – for the two men had spared many times against one another. In the heat of combat, Sandar kept part of his focus on the warrior maiden. He did not know her, but he would not like seeing her entrails spilled on the black soil.

She was nimble, but not as skilled as the soldiers she was up against. Fighting off two formidable warriors was almost too much for her, but when a third came into the attack, Sandar yanked the knife from its scabbard and hurled it toward the fight, its blade striking one of the soldiers in the back of the head.

"You are good with a blade, I will give you that," Sigrin said keeping his balance. "But you are no match for the army of Dorvainia."

The Sprite let out a cry and when Sandar turned his attention toward her, she had fallen to the ground – her attackers looming over her. Sandar snarled, gritted his teeth. For him this fight had gone on far too long. With a shift of his footing, he kicked Sigrin in the mid-section and drew his blade to the right, swung the sword in his hand and used the hilt of the weapon, clobbering his trusted officer in the head, knocking him unconscious. He couldn't bring himself to kill his friend.

Despite the death of his fellow soldiers, Sandar refused to be stifled with his men's death. It was a battle and in battles people died. Even though it was a good bet Grenvere sent Sigrin and his men here to die, for the sorcerer couldn't take the chance of Sandar dying, it was Grenvere's only link to maintaining the facade that he was General Sandar.

Withdrawing from Sigrin, Sandar dove into the fray, landing between the Sprite and her two attackers. He caught their steels against his, and deflected their attacked with ease, drawing his broadsword up slicing through the gut of one of the men. His death cry echoed throughout the forest, but before he dropped to the ground, Sandar had punched the other man square in the face – the soldier staggered back, and the Sprite tossed her axe, its sharp edge lodging in the man's chest.

Sandar looked down at the warrior maiden, but before he could ask her, she said, "Are you all right?" He reached down a hand to her, and with her lilt hand in his, he lifted her up.

The Sprite walked away from Sandar, surveying the battlefield. "These were your friends," she said turning toward him.

Sandar held his response. There were no words for how he felt. How could there be? He swore to protect the Empire, anyway he knew how. If this was the only way available to him, then so be it.

"What now?" the Sprite asked.

"Now, I continue with what I started. I find and kill Grenvere, end this madness," Sandar said, but spun on the heels of his boots when he heard, "You will not have to look far. I am here."

Grenvere floated inches from the ground, his robes flowing in the wind, his hands outstretched. "This has been a long time coming," he said. "I have sacrificed many souls so I might come to power." Beneath his robes, the tormented faces of his victims appeared. Their screams were deafening, their eyes filled with horror. "I killed so many to find my way here, to spread an army across my homelands, to make then pay for what they did to me. It would not have been possible, if it weren't for you."

"It's true then," Sandar said. "You need me alive, otherwise you would have killed me and not sent me to the dungeon."

"I must maintain the illusion. I must allow your army to believe they are following the great General Sandar. I control your king, your army and even your wife has willingly laid before me."

"You, filth...!" Sandar rushed forward disregarding a warning from the Sprite.

Grenvere outstretched a hand in his direction, and whispered a simple spell, eclipsing Sandar in a force of energy. "I may not be able to kill you General Sandar. But that doesn't mean I can't put you out of the way, so I might continue with my retribution. One day, if we meet again, I promise, I will kill you."

Sandar had to force out his reply, "Or I, you."

"Defiant to the last," Grenvere said with a sinister smile. His form changing, morphing into the image of Sandar. "Goodbye General."

"Sandar..." the Sprite shouted, rushing toward him, leaping in his direction and in that split second, they were expelled out of the Bragnor Forest, transported along a beam of light – images of land, water, sea and air flung by them at an alarming rate until... Sandar and the Sprite slammed into the ground, on the outskirts of a great desert where greenery and sand meet. The air was arid and harsh, the sky blue as an ocean and the sun hot as burning flame.

"Where... what... why?" the Sprite said in amazement, by the tone of her voice she was unable to comprehend what happened.

Sandar stood at the cusp of endless sand and said, "He couldn't kill me, so he disposed of me the only way he could."

"Where are we?" the Sprite asked.

"If I'm right, and that's a big *if,* we are on the edge of the Stryation Desert," Sandar said. "Two thousand leagues from the Dorvainian Empire and a lifetime of travel."

The Sprite joined Sandar looking out at the dunes ahead of them. "What do we do?"

"What we have to, to survive," Sandar said. "And find a way back home, as quickly as we can."

"But, that's impossible."

"As impossible as invading my memories?" Sandar asked holding up his broadsword. "You can stay here if you like. But I have a wife waiting for me at home. I intend on seeing her again, and planting this sword into that worm, Grenvere, or die trying."

"I'll go with you, if you don't mind, General."

Sandar thought about that for a moment. Her words sinking in. "You were right, when you first met me," he said looking at her. "I *am* a barbarian. I have to be if we are going to survive this journey. Right now, General Drapa Sandar is waging war on the other side of the world. I am not that man... not anymore. I have no name. Not until I take it back from him, and undo everything he has done."

"What if you can't?" the Sprite asked.

He didn't answer that, and instead said, "Let's go, we have a long journey ahead of us."

As he and the young warrior maiden set out, he put away his memories of his past life and focused on who he was now and what he had to do...

He traveled east. The Barbarian with no name.

ABOUT THE AUTHOR

Charles F. Millhouse is an Award-Winning Author and Publisher. He published his first book in 1999, and he hasn't looked back. He has written over forty published works including novels and short stories. From the 1930's adventures of Captain Hawklin – through the gritty paranormal old west town of New Kingdom – to the far-off future in the Origin Trilogy. Charles' imagination is boundless. He breathes life into his characters, brings worlds alive and sends his readers on journeys they won't soon forget.

Charles lives in Southeastern, Ohio with his wife and two sons.

Visit stormgatepress.com for more details.

Printed in Great Britain
by Amazon